José Moselli

The Curious Crimes of John Strobbins

cinderoracle.com

Contents

Foreword

Long before the term *antihero* became fashionable, José Moselli was crafting brilliant, morally ambiguous characters who blurred the line between justice and crime, genius and scoundrel. Moselli, a French writer of the early 20th century, remains one of the great unsung masters of the adventure and detective genres. His stories, which originally appeared in serialized form in European newspapers and magazines, thrilled readers with their fast-paced plots, biting humor, and a protagonist who was as much a philosopher of the street as he was a thief.

Born in 1882, Moselli was both a keen observer of human nature and a craftsman of tightly plotted tales. His fiction reflected the turbulence of his times: the cynicism of the Belle Époque, the social inequalities of the industrial era, and the fascination with modernity and technology. His signature character — here presented as John Strobbins — is emblematic of this spirit: an ingenious criminal who exposes the hypocrisy of society's so-called respectable elite even as he enriches himself at their expense.

The three stories in this volume which have been translated into English for the first time — *An Inexplicable Disappearance*, *The Margarita*, and *The Amateur* — showcase Moselli at his best: a master of misdirection and irony, whose tales deliver not just suspense but a sly commentary on greed, pride, and the illusion of authority.

This edition seeks to introduce Moselli's work to a new generation of readers, with a translation and presentation that preserve his wry wit and brisk pacing while rendering his prose accessible to contemporary audiences.

As you turn the page, prepare to meet John Strobbins — a character who, despite his crimes, somehow earns our admiration — and to enter Moselli's world: one of clever schemes, darkly comic twists, and a sharp eye on the follies of human ambition.

— *Lucius Madison*

I

An Inexplicable Disappearance

I

$\mathbf{U}$nder what circumstances — and how — the bank courier John Morris vanished was impossible to determine.

At forty-two years old, nearly six feet tall, and known never to drink, John Morris had worked at the New Century Bank of San Francisco ever since his arrival in America fifteen years earlier. His superiors valued his honesty and precision. On several occasions he had been entrusted with delicate assignments, and he always acquitted himself honorably. He was the man routinely chosen for the largest collections.

On that day, having completed his rounds, he was supposed to have had in his satchel a little more than two hundred fifteen thousand dollars — nearly one million francs — yet he did not reappear, neither at the bank nor at his home on Louisiana Avenue.

And yet, he had carried out all his collections, and in the exact order laid out by his manager. At three-thirty he had stopped at the Union Bank and cashed a draft for three hundred forty-seven dollars — and after that, his trail disappeared.

It was as if John Morris had simply vanished into thin air.

He was seen leaving the Union Bank — and that was all.

When a courier disappears, there are two usual explanations: flight with the money, or an ambush.

Both seemed highly unlikely here. John Morris, a thrifty and orderly man, already had nearly eighteen thousand dollars — about seventy-five thousand francs — on deposit at the New Century, the fruit of his savings and some lucky investments made on the advice of the bank's director, who had taken an interest in him.

If Morris had wanted to flee — which would have been absurd, given that he was already wealthy — he would surely have withdrawn his own funds first. No, the idea of flight was simply implausible.

John Morris was a quiet man, not someone who would risk a life of hard labor for a crime.

And an ambush? Hardly likely in the streets of San Francisco.

The Union Bank, where Morris was last seen, stood near the Stock Exchange, right in the heart of the business district: an assault there was impossible at four in the afternoon.

And yet, the fact remained: John Morris had disappeared — and with him, two hundred fifteen thousand dollars.

The staff of San Francisco's various train stations were questioned. None of them recalled seeing the courier. The same went for the crews of the many ferries that plied the bay.

James Mollescott, chief of police for San Francisco, sent his sharpest detectives to look for the missing man. They returned empty-handed.

Seeing this, the director of the New Century Bank resorted to the old and often-used tactic: he offered a reward of twenty thousand dollars — one hundred thousand francs — to anyone who could provide news of John Morris.

Naturally, this announcement had the immediate effect of bringing a horde of beggars and opportunists swarming to the bank, each claiming to have seen the cashier at this or that place, at this or that time.

These claims were checked one by one, and all were found to be false.

And the fate of John Morris remained a mystery.

Samuel Baker, director of the New Century Bank, grew resentful.

He was a suspicious and hot-tempered man. To his mind, there was no doubt: the cashier, a thief and an ingrate, had run off.

Two hundred fifteen thousand dollars — half the year's profits! Samuel Baker could not get over it.

His perplexity only deepened fifteen days after John Morris's disappearance, when he received the following letter at his private residence:

Sir,

Confident in your promise to pay twenty thousand dollars — one hundred thousand francs — to anyone who could, with proof, inform you of Mr. John Morris's fate, I set out to investigate. After considerable difficulty, and at the cost of real and serious danger, I have discovered what became of Mr. Morris.

I am prepared to share the results of my investigation, on three conditions:

First, that you receive me in person, without witnesses, and in a place safe from prying eyes.

Second, that you promise — whatever happens — never to reveal my name.

Third, that the twenty thousand dollars be deposited today with the clerk of the court. If my information proves correct — and it will — you will sign a simple receipt allowing me to collect it.

If these conditions are agreeable to you, please place the following notice in tomorrow's *Californian Herald*, in the classified section:

"Agreed. Come at 10:03."

I will present myself under the name Georges Murdstone.

Samuel Baker reread this strange letter several times.

It seemed serious enough. Still, the precautions his correspondent demanded did not sit well with him...

No doubt it was one of the accomplices — either of the cashier, if he were guilty, or of his killer, if he had been murdered.

The best course of action, then, was to notify the police, pretend to accept, and have the man arrested. Once in jail, he would talk — and Baker would save himself a hundred thousand francs.

The banker rubbed his hands and, without delay, sent the following notice to the *Californian Herald*:

"Agreed. Come today, Thursday, at 10:03."

Then, quite pleased with himself, he wrote a long letter to James Mollescott, chief of police for San Francisco, informing him that the next morning the presumed killer of John Morris would present himself at the bank, and asking that four strong detectives be sent to apprehend him.

The clock read half past eleven in the morning by the time Samuel Baker was done. He carefully sealed his letter, had his hat brought, and went himself to drop the missive in the nearest mailbox.

II

A cheerful sun gilded the streets, and his spirits were high. Delighted at the thought of catching the assassin — and especially at the prospect of recovering the two hundred fifteen thousand dollars — Samuel Baker, who usually dined at home, decided to treat himself to a meal at a restaurant.

Smiling, he entered the Carlton Hotel, settled at a table, asked for the menu, and began planning a fine meal.

It seemed many others had had the same idea that day, for the Carlton soon filled up and every table was occupied.

That was why Samuel Baker made no objection when the maître d'hôtel respectfully approached and said:

"Would it bother you, sir, if this gentleman took the seat opposite you? There are so many guests today."

The banker, who was perusing the menu, looked up and saw a well-dressed young man waiting for his answer.

"Not at all," he said. "Please, have a seat."

"You are really too kind," murmured the newcomer. Slowly, he sat down opposite Samuel Baker.

"You see, sir, nowadays everyone eats in restaurants… Understandable, isn't it? There are no more servants."

Samuel Baker agreed with this sentiment. In his opinion, not only were servants hard to find these days, but good employees were as well. He even cited examples of recent dishonesties committed at various banks in the city.

"Oh, you must know quite a bit about that," replied the stranger. "If I'm not mistaken, you are Mr. Samuel Baker, director of the New Century Bank?"

"I am."

"Well then, I'm glad chance seated me here with you. You see, I myself am Mr. Georges Murdstone!"

"I don't recall…"

"Oh yes… Allow me to explain. But first, a warning: if you make a move, if you say a single suspicious word — you understand me, don't you? — I'll blow your head off. And don't think they'll catch me. The car waiting outside is ready to take me away at a moment's notice."

As he spoke, Georges Murdstone moved his hand slightly, and the banker, terrified, caught sight of a small Browning pistol strapped to his forearm by some ingenious mechanism, its dark barrel aimed right at him.

"Sir…" began Baker.

"Let me speak!"

"Do you understand who I am? Yes, don't you — the man who wrote to you this morning. I suspected you'd try to wriggle out of your commitments. I looked into you before writing. But this isn't the time to argue. A bit more of this carp, dear sir? It's excellent."

The waiter arrived just then with a platter of roast. Georges Murdstone, smiling, kept his arm perfectly still. The banker didn't move.

"No, thank you," Baker said. "No more fish."

The waiter removed the carp, set the roast on the table, changed the plates, and discreetly withdrew.

"I'll continue," murmured Georges Murdstone, in a low voice and without taking his eyes off Baker. "I've been tracking the killer for ten days now, and I don't intend to be cheated. So, suspecting your trickery, I waited for you outside your bank. I followed you and saw you slip this into a mailbox."

Murdstone produced, to the banker's horror, the letter he had written to James Mollescott.

Murdstone smiled.

"Child's play… I fished it out with a stick coated in glue, and read it. Thanks for that. But I bear you no grudge — business is business, isn't it? And it's only natural to try to save twenty thousand dollars when you can. Still, since I have no wish to tangle with the police, I'll accompany you to your bank. Once we're alone, I'll tell you everything about what happened to your man. You see, I'm a loyal fellow. I'm not changing my offer.

"Now, once we're at the New Century Bank, don't try to have me arrested — you'd regret it. I won't press the point, and I'm so sure of your loyalty that I'm ready to follow you whenever you like."

The waiter brought coffee and cigars. Murdstone took a Havana, struck a match, and, after crumpling Baker's letter to Mollescott, set it alight and gallantly offered it so Baker could light his cigar.

In one gulp, Georges Murdstone drained his coffee. The banker imitated him and stood up.

"If you'd like to take my car?" Murdstone offered.

"No... thank you... I prefer to walk a little after meals. Aids digestion."

"Oh, I've no intention of kidnapping you," Murdstone replied with a mocking grin.

He handed the waiter a twenty-dollar bill.

"Keep the change," he said.

The two men left. Ten minutes later, they entered the New Century Bank.

"I'm not here for anyone," Samuel Baker told his secretary.

Samuel Baker and Georges Murdstone, walking side by side like old friends, arrived at the New Century Bank's reception room. Samuel Baker closed the door, threw the bolts, and said to his companion:

"You can speak, sir. We are alone, safe from indiscretion."

"Too kind of you," Murdstone replied. "Your offer makes me feel like a fool — though I assure you I'm not. This room, my dear Mr. Baker, is where your bank's board of directors meets... and it's designed so that from your private office you can hear every word spoken here."

"Sir..."

"Let's not waste time. I promised to tell you — you alone, understand me-what became of your cashier. If you want to know, take me to your office."

"I don't receive anyone there, sir."

"In that case, we have nothing more to say to each other."

Samuel Baker looked at Georges Murdstone. The latter was calm and determined.

"But still," the banker murmured, "I don't quite see…"

"Why I insist on speaking with you alone? Because my revelations could bring me a great deal of trouble if anyone knew where they came from."

"Very well then… come with me."

III

Certainly, Samuel Baker's curiosity must have been strong to lead him to usher this stranger into his office. The office itself was protected by a reinforced concrete corridor and three successive armored doors. There were no windows — just a thin air vent and two incandescent lamps to allow one to see and breathe. This was where Baker kept his archives.

Following the banker, Georges Murdstone entered and sat on a steel chair. The only furniture was a painted metal desk and two chairs. Against the walls stood three enormous closed safes.

"I'm listening, sir," declared Samuel Baker after locking the doors.

"Thank you. Here's the story: your bank courier, John Morris, was murdered — and under extraordinary circumstances.

"On his route, as you'll recall, he was supposed to collect a check from Mr. Julius Cander, wasn't he? He arrived at Cander's apartment just before three o'clock. Cander had left the necessary money with his valet to settle the check.

"When John Morris rang the bell, I was already in the apartment. You're probably wondering what I was doing there, eh? With some friends, I was in the process of moving a Murillo painting that interested me greatly.

"Everything was just about finished, and I was replacing the Murillo with a rather well-done copy — good enough that Cander never noticed. I knew the valet was busy in the pantry, so the sound of the bell annoyed me.

"I left my friends to finish and pressed my eye to the keyhole — I'm a curious man, you see. I watched the valet, Paul Brener, open the door and let in your courier. Morris came in, set his satchel on a table, and began extracting the check from Cander's papers.

"As he did so, Brener pulled a small iron hammer from his apron and struck Morris a terrible blow to the back of the neck. Without a cry, Morris collapsed on the carpet — quite efficiently done.

"Brener, a strong fellow, hoisted the body onto his back, pushed open a nearby door with his foot, and carried it through. I followed, fascinated by his composure. Brener took the elevator to the top floor — the attic of the building.

"Of course, I knew the house well — it was my workplace, after all. I noticed, incidentally, that Brener had also taken the satchel along with the body — how prudent of him.

"I didn't linger. I took another elevator and quickly reached the twelfth floor. Following the noise Brener made, I saw him enter his own room and close the door. I tried to peek through the keyhole, but he'd blocked it.

"Fortunately, I had a small hand drill — it took ten seconds to bore a tiny, silent hole. Through it, I placed the lens of my miniature camera and, frame by frame, shot twenty-four photographs of what followed.

"I brought you copies of them all.

"You'll see: Brener undressed Morris, immersed his naked body in a cylindrical vat in the center of the room, then dressed himself in the dead man's clothes, even applying makeup to resemble him perfectly. He tucked a soft cap and a thin rubberized raincoat into Morris's satchel and left.

"I barely had time to withdraw and hide at the end of the corridor behind a large pine wardrobe. I watched Brener emerge and take the elevator.

"As soon as he was gone, I entered his room and saw the large lead vat filled with sulfuric acid, in which the body was dissolving. Ingenious, wasn't it?

"The rest was easy to understand: disguised as the courier — and nobody looks too closely at the end of the month as long as the papers are in order — Brener continued Morris's route.

"At four-thirty I saw him return, wearing the rubber raincoat and soft cap he'd brought in the satchel. Back in his room, he stripped off the disguise and dropped it, along with the empty satchel, into the acid bath.

"Then he put his valet's livery back on.

"You can guess the rest. In the following days, Brener quietly disposed of the acid and its dissolved remains in bottles, likely cut up the lead vat and threw the pieces into the sea.

"I think that's ample information, don't you? And here are the twenty-four photographs I mentioned. Surely worth the twenty thousand dollars you promised."

Smiling, Georges Murdstone handed Baker a stack of twenty-four small, remarkably clear photographs. They depicted everything Murdstone had described.

Baker examined them silently, then locked them away in one of the enormous safes.

Then he said:

"Twenty-four photos, at a hundred dollars apiece — that's twenty-four hundred dollars, and not a cent more."

Murdstone bowed.

"You don't keep your promises, Mr. Baker," he said. "Very well. Pay me the twenty-four hundred. After all, I worked 'as an amateur' that day."

Baker regretted not offering less. With a sigh, he drew twenty-four one-hundred-dollar bills from his wallet and handed them over.

Murdstone pocketed the money without counting it.

"And above all, Mr. Baker," he added, "not a word about me to anyone — you gave me your word."

"Have no fear," said Baker, not noticing Murdstone's mocking smile.

"Shall we go out?"

"Gladly."

The two men passed through the three armored doors. Once back in the main office, Murdstone saluted Baker, walked quickly to the exit, and melted into the crowd.

"I should have had him arrested," grumbled Baker.

He leapt for the telephone and immediately called James Mollescott at the police department to relay what he had just learned.

Six detectives rushed to Julius Cander's hotel.

No one had seen Paul Brener since morning.

The police broke down the door to his room and found his body hanging from a rope.

On the wooden table lay a typewritten note:

Murderer of John Morris — the police know everything. The banknotes are no longer where you left them. It is immoral for a murderer to profit from his crime.

Apparently panicked, Brener had tried to flee, but finding the money gone and himself lost, he hanged himself.

Indeed, the two hundred fifteen thousand dollars were never recovered.

And despite Baker's statement to the police that very day about Georges Murdstone, the man was never found.

A week later, Samuel Baker was called to the telephone.

A voice said:

"Don't forget, Mr. Baker, that you still owe me seventeen thousand six hundred dollars, which, at one hundred percent interest every twenty-four hours, now amounts to two million two hundred fifty-two thousand eight hundred dollars. I think it's best to leave it at that, don't you? I'll collect tomorrow."

The receiver clicked.

Samuel Baker merely shrugged.

He was wrong to.

IV

The disappearance of cashier John Morris — and especially the discovery and suicide of his ingenious killer, Paul Brener — had greatly stirred the people of San Francisco.

Unaware of the role played by the mysterious Georges Murdstone in the affair, the citizens of San Francisco gave full credit to the extraordinary instincts of their chief of police, James Mollescott.

Mollescott, for his part, was happy to let them believe it, pleased to see his popularity restored after the damage caused by the still-unsolved exploits of John Strobbins.

Samuel Baker, director of the New Century Bank, could have told the truth, but he didn't bother. What good would it do? The two hundred fifteen thousand dollars stolen from the cashier had vanished for good, and better not to keep talking about a matter that could only alarm the bank's clients.

Still, the mysterious Georges Murdstone weighed on his mind.

Though Baker told himself the strange man's threats were mere bluff, he remained uneasy. After Murdstone so cavalierly demanded two million two hundred fifty-two thousand eight hundred dollars over the phone, Baker disdainfully hung up the receiver — but he stood, pale, a little unsteady.

His clerks saw him light a cigar and leave the bank, his back slightly hunched. They assumed — quite reasonably — that he was shaken by the theft his cashier had suffered.

Mollescott and his detectives, meanwhile, had failed to find any trace of Georges Murdstone — or of the missing money.

The next day, Samuel Baker did not appear at the New Century Bank. When the market opened, his deputy, worried, sent someone to his home: Baker had returned there at six o'clock the previous evening, gone out again at eight — and never come back.

Alarmed, the deputy telephoned everywhere: the stock exchange, the brokers' council, the bankers' syndicate. No one had seen Baker.

Panicked and at a loss, he finally went to the police.

Admitted to James Mollescott's office, he explained the inexplicable disappearance of his director.

Mollescott nodded.

"Without saying too much," he remarked, "I'd say his disappearance seems like a consequence of his cashier's murder. Everything about this business is bizarre, and I regret we couldn't find this Murdstone — if he even exists… yes, if he exists.

"What do I know, other than what your boss told me?

"All we're sure of is that Paul Brener killed himself — and that proves little enough. Nothing truly confirms his guilt."

"His suicide!" the deputy protested.

"That remains to be seen," Mollescott replied. "In any case — just a hypothesis, mind you — perhaps Mr. Baker, facing financial troubles, conspired with his cashier. Eh? Right now, he could be far away, with the two hundred fifteen thousand dollars."

Smiling, Mollescott rubbed his hands, satisfied with his theory.

The deputy shrugged.

"Know this, Mr. Mollescott," he said, "the New Century Bank's accounts are perfectly sound — and Mr. Baker himself is worth more than two million dollars."

"Fine, fine," said Mollescott, irritated his theory had not impressed. "Rest assured, sir, we'll do what's necessary — but even wealthy men have been known to ruin themselves and run off!"

Mollescott rose, signaling that the conversation was over. The deputy bowed and left.

Alone, the chief of police returned to his paperwork.

Suddenly, reading a letter written on fine parchment stationery, he grunted in satisfaction.

"Good old Parnell! Still remembers me. Excellent idea — I'll enjoy a pleasant Sunday."

He chuckled, rang a bell, and summoned his deputy.

"My dear Brown," he said, "I'll be gone all day tomorrow, Sunday. An old friend has invited me to hunt with him on his Stockton estate. I'm leaving things in your hands. Send two of our best detectives to look for Samuel Baker."

"The director of the New Century Bank, sir?"

"The same. He's vanished."

"He's run off with the two hundred fifteen thousand dollars!"

"That's my thought exactly. So, Brown — it's settled. You're in charge."

"You can count on me, sir."

"I know I can. Anything else?"

"No, sir. Thank you."

The next morning, James Mollescott rose at dawn and arrived at the Northwestern Line station by six. The train to Stockton wasn't leaving for another half hour.

Carrying his leather-cased shotgun over his shoulder, he sat on the platform, quite cheerful.

It had been three years since he'd seen his old friend Parnell, who had left for Louisiana to tend his plantations. Now Parnell was back in Stockton, and Mollescott looked forward to a fine day of hunting.

When the train was ready, Mollescott settled into a comfortable Pullman and bought a newspaper to pass the time.

An hour later, he arrived at Stockton.

The small station was deserted. Mollescott, the only passenger to disembark, was surprised not to see Parnell waiting for him.

Instead, a man in a driver's livery — elegant yet austere — approached, saluted respectfully, and said:

"Mr. James Mollescott, I presume?"

"That's right."

"I'm Mr. Blaise Parnell's coachman. My master was taken ill last night and sends his apologies for not meeting you himself. He asked me to bring you to his cottage."

"Ah — nothing serious, I hope?" Mollescott asked, concerned.

"Oh, no… but since his time in Louisiana, Mr. Parnell has become quite sensitive to the cold."

They left the station. Outside, an elegant varnished pine gig, harnessed to a pony, stood waiting.

The coachman untied the horse, helped Mollescott climb in, then took the reins.

A fresh breeze blew, scattering wisps of white cloud across the blue sky and rustling the trees. Roosters crowed in the distance and the pony's bells jingled merrily.

Mollescott felt glad to be alive.

He set his shotgun beside him, lit a cigar, and leaned back.

The coachman, silent and dignified, drove without comment. After a moment he reached down, picked up Mollescott's shotgun, and placed it on the floor between his legs.

"There — now it won't get scratched," he said with a faint smile.

Mollescott nodded.

The pony trotted on, and more than half an hour passed. Mollescott began to find the ride tedious. He tossed aside his finished cigar and looked around.

As far as the eye could see, fields of cotton stretched across the vast plain. Not a single house broke the horizon.

Mollescott frowned.

"Are we still far from Mr. Parnell's place?" he asked.

The wind blew hard, and the coachman did not answer.

Mollescott repeated the question.

This time the coachman turned, pointed to a distant rise in the land, and said simply:

"Just over there."

"Ah — good."

Mollescott, weary from the jolting ride, lit another cigar.

But as he struck the match, the pony suddenly reared.

The jolt was so violent that Mollescott would have been thrown to the ground had the coachman not seized him firmly by the collar of his overcoat and held him in place.

Mollescott, stunned and not understanding what was happening, fell back into the seat of the carriage.

He felt an iron grip close around his throat and a terrible weight press down on his chest.

Above him he saw the mocking face of the coachman, staring down at him — and, just three centimeters from his forehead, the black muzzle of a revolver.

The coachman sneered.

"Don't move, or you're dead, James Mollescott!

"I need to have a word with you! You're going to let me put these cuffs on you — otherwise I'll have to knock you out first! Don't worry, I don't intend to harm you. I simply want to tell you a story — but I need to be sure I won't be interrupted!"

James Mollescott regained his wits. He studied the false coachman carefully and, after a couple of seconds, growled:

"May the devil take me! It's John Strobbins!"

"The very same," the man said.

V

The horse had settled down again and now stood calmly.

"What do you want from me?" Mollescott muttered through clenched teeth, seething with rage.

"First, you're going to let me put these handcuffs on you. For that, I'll need to let go of my revolver — so be warned: if you make even the slightest move, either to attack me or to run, I won't hesitate to hurt you. Do I have your word that you'll stay still?"

"No."

John Strobbins had expected that answer.

His right hand released the revolver, letting it fall to the floor of the carriage, and joined his left in tightening around the chief of police's throat.

Half-strangled, Mollescott gasped and choked. Strobbins released his throat for just a moment, only to grab his wrists instead. Mollescott gulped air greedily — once, twice — and, his strength returning, tried to struggle.

Too late.

Thin, nickel-plated steel cuffs now fastened his wrists. When he moved to free himself, they bit cruelly into his flesh, drawing a cry of pain.

"I'm truly sorry, Mr. Mollescott," said Strobbins, "but you'll admit you forced me to this. After all, it's only fair — your turn to wear the cuffs, isn't it?"

Mollescott said nothing.

"Now then," Strobbins continued, "get up and sit here beside me. I brought you all this way just to tell you a story. You'll see — it's worth the trip."

Obligingly, Strobbins helped him up and seated him on the bench beside him.

Mollescott now understood why the supposed coachman had so cheerfully relieved him of his shotgun earlier.

With a click of his tongue, Strobbins set the horse in motion again. He guided the carriage down a narrow path through the cotton fields and, after some three hundred meters, stopped, climbed down, and tied the horse to a nearby tree.

"There, now we can talk," he said. "Get down."

With a firm hand, Strobbins helped Mollescott down, showing him the revolver.

"Don't try to run — or else…"

Mollescott merely shrugged and said nothing.

"Let's sit over there, shall we?" Strobbins went on, pointing to a grassy mound.

Mollescott nodded and sat beside him.

Strobbins sighed in contentment.

"Ah, I'm glad we finally got here. Honestly, I was afraid you'd miss the train. But here we are — and I'm delighted.

"It's ten o'clock now, and I don't want to take up too much of your time. We're about two miles from a village where you can get lunch.

"As for your friend Parnell — the one whose name I used to write you — don't worry. He's still in Baton Rouge, Louisiana, in excellent health. I had the pleasure of seeing him just a few days ago.

"Now then — let me tell you why I wanted this little chat.

"Yesterday afternoon, the deputy from the New Century Bank came to see you, asking you to investigate his missing director, didn't he?

"Well, I brought you here simply to tell you where Samuel Baker is — and to make you a witness to the legitimacy of what I did.

"When John Morris disappeared, Samuel Baker promised a twenty-thousand-dollar reward to anyone who could bring certain information about him.

"Trusting in his word — well, not really trusting, but trusting enough — I wrote him a letter offering to provide him with all the details about his cashier if he would meet me privately.

"Well, the scoundrel published an ad in the Californian Herald agreeing to my terms — then immediately ran to you.

"I never got a letter about that," Mollescott interrupted.

"I know — because I intercepted it. I'd been watching Baker and used a sticky rod to fish his letter to you out of the mailbox before it was collected.

"Anyway — no time to waste. I had a job waiting in Pasadena. So I beat him to the meeting. I caught up with Baker at the restaurant where he was lunching and convinced him to take me straight to the bank. I had a plan.

"With a revolver hidden in my sleeve, I forced him into his private office. Once there, I gave him proof of his cashier's murder — and even a few photographs. There were twenty of them; I still have the negatives. So he knew the whole story: what happened to Morris, how it happened, and who did it.

"I asked him for the promised twenty thousand dollars. He laughed in my face and begrudgingly handed me just twenty-four hundred — not even enough to pay a day's wages to my men. I said nothing, took it, and left.

"But I took with me wax molds of every lock I'd passed through.

"With those, I spent eight days having keys and tools made.

"Then I called Samuel Baker — he probably told you about me, as George Murdstone? — and informed him he owed me seventeen thousand six hundred dollars, plus eight days' interest at a hundred percent per day, which came to exactly two million two hundred fifty-two thousand eight hundred dollars. I added that, not wanting to ruin him completely, I would soon come to settle the debt.

"He didn't answer. That was his mistake.

"That very evening, using the keys I'd had made, I slipped into the bank after hours. I entered the vault with his office and safes. With my electric torch, I opened the safe where I'd seen Baker lock up the other keys. I drilled it open, took the key ring, opened one of the big safes, and removed exactly two million two hundred fifty-two thousand eight hundred dollars' worth of securities.

"I hid the bundle and drilled tiny holes in the safe walls — you'll see why in a moment.

"Then I packed up my tools and hid behind a metal file cabinet.

"I waited. My patience paid off.

"Around ten o'clock — as he did every night — Baker came to make his nightly inspection. He was cautious, that one. But not cautious enough.

"The moment he entered the vault, I jumped him.

"With a silk scarf, I gagged him. He was so stunned he barely struggled. I tied him to a chair.

"'It's me,' I told him. 'George Murdstone, alias John Strobbins. As promised, I've come to collect principal and interest. Not a cent more — I'm an honest man, unlike you.'

"His eyes bulged. It made me laugh, but I was not there to amuse myself.

"'Now,' I told him, 'to punish you for wasting my time, I'll waste yours. I'm going to lock you in one of your own safes — don't worry, you won't suffocate, I drilled holes. You'll have time to reflect on the cost of breaking your word. In three days, I'll have you let out.'

"He would have begged, no doubt, if he hadn't been gagged.

"I laid him in the safe, shut the door, took my bundle of securities, and left the New Century Bank without a hitch.

"The next morning I sold the securities. Baker owes me nothing now.

"There you have it.

"I sent you, last night, some prints of the photographs from the cashier's murder. I sent copies to the press as well — they prove Baker did indeed owe me the money I took.

"I bear him no grudge.

"Thanks to him, I've just enjoyed a pleasant hour in your company.

"I hope we meet again."

"You can count on it," Mollescott growled.

"So can I."

John Strobbins glanced at his watch.

"Eleven o'clock!" he exclaimed. "Time flies in good company. I don't want to keep you from your lunch, Mr. Mollescott. Will you follow me?"

John Strobbins stood, and silently the police chief did the same.

The two men returned to the road. Strobbins pointed toward a spot on the horizon and said:

"Just behind that little hill is the village of Jump Rocks. There are excellent inns there — the Red Devil among them. Enjoy your meal!"

With a quick gesture, John Strobbins removed the handcuffs from James Mollescott's wrists and leapt back to his carriage.

He raised his revolver and added:

"I'm one of those who prefers not to be escorted. Farewell!"

James Mollescott merely shrugged and stood still.

He watched John Strobbins untie his horse, jump into the carriage, and disappear at full gallop.

Then Mollescott turned toward the place the detective-burglar had indicated and, three-quarters of an hour later, arrived at the village of Jump Rocks.

He ate lunch and left for San Francisco immediately afterward.

He went straight to police headquarters, summoned a locksmith on the spot, and, accompanied by the locksmith and two detectives, made his way to the New Century Bank.

John Strobbins had told the truth: Samuel Baker, half-starved, gagged, and bound, lay inside a safe, breathing only through three tiny holes.

He was quickly freed from the safe, his bonds cut. They fed him, massaged him, and revived him.

At last, comforted and regaining his strength, he murmured:

"What a shame I couldn't have partnered with a fellow like that — we'd have done wonders together…"

James Mollescott handed him a piece of paper.

"Here, Mr. Baker," he said. "I just found this on your desk."

"Give it here."

Samuel Baker opened the envelope. Inside was a sheet of paper, on which was written:

Received from Mr. Samuel Baker the sum of $2,252,800 in securities, payment for information and documents provided by me.

Account settled as of this date.

San Francisco, April 18, 19—

JOHN STROBBINS

II

The Margarita

I

The manner in which John Strobbins managed to steal the marvelous pearl known as "The Margarita" has remained a mystery to this day.

And although some of the most cunning police detectives in the world — tempted both by the hundred-thousand-dollar reward offered by President Shaft and by the prestige of such a capture — exhausted all their deductive skills and professional instincts trying to recover the priceless pearl, it has never reappeared.

A short note, published in the *Washington Sun*, informed the public that The Margarita was now in the possession of John Strobbins.

A photograph, sent by the famous detective-burglar himself and reproduced by the newspaper, showed the inestimable pearl, authenticating Strobbins's claim.

Before recounting the circumstances of how The Margarita was stolen, it's worth summarizing the story of this unique gem.

The Margarita was first found by a poor fisherman near Margarita Island, off the coast of Venezuela.

When discovered, The Margarita was what's called a baroque pearl — as large as a man's fist but marred by grayish blemishes that dulled its luster.

It was purchased by Señor Elias Agostino Barquisimelo, a Venezuelan nobleman who, for his own private and particular reasons, sought to curry favor with General Castro, then president of the Republic of Venezuela. He presented the pearl to Castro as a gift — its value lying more in its size than in its luster.

Some time later, when General Castro needed coal to refuel the republic's sole navy ship, he traded the pearl to an American coal merchant, John Hanger, in exchange for three hundred tons of anthracite.

On examining the pearl and seeing the flaws that marred it, Hanger had a brilliant idea. With a single hammer blow, he shattered the imperfect outer layers of nacre and revealed a stunning, walnut-sized pearl with a luminous, gentle sheen.

For several moments, John Hanger stood dumbfounded at having uncovered such a treasure. Then, in true American fashion, he calculated its value: several million dollars.

Two days later, John Hanger boarded a steamer at La Guaira, bound for New York, carrying The Margarita hidden in his belt.

The marvelous pearl, displayed under the watch of six detectives in the window of a Broadway jeweler, was eventually purchased for three million dollars by Mr. Jim Snowboots, the sugar-cane king.

Three weeks later, Jim Snowboots died, leaving the precious Margarita to the National Museum in his hometown of Washington.

When the news broke, Mr. Herbert Roston, curator of the National Museum, wasted no time in finding a secure place to display the magnificent Margarita.

At the same time, John Strobbins was already thinking of stealing it.

It was a daunting undertaking — fraught with difficulties, perhaps impossible. But let us proceed in the natural order of events.

A special chamber was prepared for The Margarita, located at the center of the National Museum, with only two exits: a pair of bronze doors and a skylight protected by a sturdy steel grille.

Despite its value, the beautiful Margarita could hardly justify occupying the room alone, so Herbert Roston added an antique statue found in Athens and several celebrated pieces of goldwork.

Once the display was complete, Mr. Roston rightly thought that the Margarita Room deserved to be inaugurated with some ceremony.

After all — *the biggest, finest pearl in the world!*

President Shaft agreed to be the first to admire the now-famous pearl. On July 1st, the day of the inauguration, a large crowd gathered to examine the marvel.

Now it's time to recount the exact and detailed circumstances of the Margarita's disappearance.

A few minutes past ten o'clock that morning, President Shaft arrived at the National Museum, accompanied by the Governor of the District of Columbia, the mayors of Philadelphia and New York, and about twenty senators.

Herbert Roston, flanked by his six assistant curators, was waiting at the entrance.

He stepped forward and, in carefully chosen words, thanked the president for the honor he was paying the National Museum.

President Shaft smiled.

"You are too kind, Mr. Roston," he said. "Let's see this famous pearl, shall we?"

Beaming with importance, the curator bowed and courteously led the president inside.

Surrounded by governors and senators, the president followed Roston through the vestibule — decorated with green plants for the occasion — across the Hall of Independence Relics, and finally into the Margarita Room.

It was an oval room, with stucco walls painted in fresco and a white marble floor.

On pedestals stood several somewhat mutilated statuettes, and in display cases, various ancient jewels no one paid much attention to.

All eyes were fixed on the pearl.

It rested on a black satin cushion atop a bronze pedestal at the center of the room. Sunlight streaming through the skylight made it glow softly.

"As you can see, Mr. President," said the curator, "this magnificent pearl is by far the largest in the world. It weighs exactly 1,153 carats, and its luster is incomparable!"

President Shaft inclined his head.

Around the pedestal, the senators and governors gathered, some of them pale at the thought of the gem's enormous value. They craned their necks and nodded silently.

"Here," Roston continued, pointing to four stout men standing silently by the pedestal, "are the guards assigned to watch over the Margarita. In addition, the pearl will be enclosed in a thick crystal case — which will allow it to be admired while protecting it from dust and thieves."

"Well — it's certainly worth it," remarked President Shaft. "Though it would be hard to sell anyway!"

He checked his watch and concluded:

"My thanks, Mr. Roston, for your courtesy — and my compliments on the art and taste you've shown in placing this beautiful pearl in a setting worthy of it."

The curator bowed, flattered.

President Shaft moved slowly toward the door as his entourage, their initial awe fading, began murmuring among themselves about the admirable Margarita.

Everyone had left the room, and Herbert Roston, last to remain, was just about to close the door when he turned back — and saw that the shimmering spot of light on the black satin cushion was gone.

His blood ran cold.

He sprang to the pedestal: The Margarita was no longer there!

II

With a quick glance at the marble floor, he convinced himself that it hadn't simply fallen.

He ran to President Shaft, who was chatting with the Governor of New York and several senators in the adjoining hall.

"Mr. President," he mumbled, "someone has stolen The Margarita!"

A wave of astonishment swept through the room.

Behind the curator of the National Museum, the four guards assigned to watch the pearl stood looking pitiful, confirming their superior's words by their dejected expressions.

President Shaft raised his head and fixed his gray eyes on the hapless official.

"Someone has stolen The Margarita?" he said. "Who? How? It can't have gotten far in any case!"

These words were spoken loud enough for the entire gathering to hear. For an instant, an awkward silence reigned.

Thomas Glifford, senator from Wisconsin, standing beside the president, cried out:

"If The Margarita isn't there anymore, then it's been stolen! We must get to the bottom of this. As for me, I'm willing to be searched — it won't take long; I've got nothing but my jacket and shirt!"

Herbert Roston, deeply embarrassed, said nothing.

President Shaft turned to his entourage.

"Come, gentlemen," he said, "let's go back to the Margarita Room. Perhaps the pearl simply rolled into a corner."

The curator of the National Museum didn't reply, but his face betrayed a hopeless disbelief.

Surrounded by the four guards, he re-entered the Margarita Room.

President Shaft, followed by the governors and senators — none of whom had left his side — entered as well.

In just a few moments, everyone was convinced: the pearl was no longer in the room.

So now what?

President Shaft looked around him. He saw Marc Carters, senator from Illinois; Robert Shum, from Kentucky; Nathaniel Bordson, from Colorado; James Hunter, from Idaho; Peter Hornsby, from Florida; James Billiken, from Texas; John Camstower, from Massachusetts.

He saw Albert Sloan, governor of the District of Columbia; Samuel Vickers and Charles Breston, mayors of New York and Philadelphia.

All of them he had known for many years.

They were perfect gentlemen, the poorest among them worth several million dollars.

They were beyond suspicion.

Over the course of his colorful life, President Shaft had seen all manner of things — as the saying goes. He quickly made up his mind.

"Mr. Herbert Roston, The Margarita is gone. Find it! You have my deepest regrets — and these gentlemen's as well. I wish you a speedy success.

"Come, gentlemen."

With that, the president turned toward the door, and, followed by his entourage, departed — leaving poor Herbert Roston speechless.

The four guards, as stricken as their chief, stood motionless, arms hanging at their sides.

One of them took a step toward the door.

That was enough to snap Herbert Roston out of his stupor.

"No one move!" he ordered. "I'm going to search everyone! Hands up!"

III

The four men raised their arms in unison.

Herbert Roston, feverish, searched their pockets.

He found some plugs of chewing tobacco, a few pennies, dirty handkerchiefs, bunches of keys, and a pipe. But no pearl.

"Strip," he ordered.

With faintly ironic expressions, the guards removed their clothing, which the curator of the National Museum examined again.

He had to admit they contained nothing.

"Fine," he grumbled. "You can get dressed."

The four men obeyed.

But where on earth was The Margarita?

Since none of President Shaft's guests could possibly be suspected, it had to be one of the guards.

But where had he hidden the pearl? In his stomach? It was far too big to swallow.

The pearl had to still be in the room — but where?

Once again, Herbert Roston searched every corner, moved statuettes and display cases.

In vain.

At last, defeated, he called the police. He resigned himself to making the disappearance of the incomparable pearl public.

Detective Ned Carver arrived at the National Museum a few minutes later.

He questioned the four guards, then had Herbert Roston recount, minute by minute, the various incidents of the presidential visit. After a brief moment of reflection, he concluded:

"No doubt about it — John Strobbins pulled this off."

"Then the pearl is lost?"

"I'm afraid so."

"But the president stated plainly that he's known all the people who accompanied him for years!"

"Well, then — Strobbins must have disguised himself as one of them! Did you count them? How many were with the president?"

"I… couldn't say… fifteen or twenty at most."

"Fifteen or twenty? You'd better try to remember all their names. I'll pay them each a visit."

"I'll do my best," Herbert Roston said.

Ned Carver didn't reply. He gave the curator a suspicious look, then raised his eyes and suddenly exclaimed:

"Are you sure the pearl wasn't thrown up into the skylight?"

Herbert Roston shrugged, annoyed by the detective's insinuations.

"No," he said. "Anyway, come with me to the roof — you'll see the skylight is protected by a tight mesh and solid bars."

"Let's see," Ned Carver said.

He had to admit it: the skylight was intact.

He questioned the four guards again, but they could only repeat what they'd already said.

The affair became more and more mysterious.

That afternoon, Herbert Roston managed — after wracking his memory — to draw up a list of President Shaft's guests.

Ned Carver visited each of them and managed to reconstruct the exact and complete list of those who had accompanied the president to the museum.

He questioned them all — but got no closer to an answer.

A month of investigation passed, and The Margarita was still not recovered.

For a few days, the newspapers made much of the mysterious disappearance — then moved on to other topics.

Herbert Roston was dismissed.

The first act of his successor was to redesign the room that had once held The Margarita.

A block of gold, of extraordinary purity and extracted in the Klondike by an American prospector, was placed in the crystal case once destined for the vanished pearl.

And the public was once again allowed into the room — to admire the precious metal in place of The Margarita.

Herbert Roston didn't have to wait long for his revenge.

Three days after the reopening of the Margarita Room — as the public stubbornly continued to call it — the *Washington Sun* published the following sensational article:

HOW OUR MUSEUMS ARE GUARDED

It would seem that after the disappearance of the precious Margarita, our museums ought to have instituted active and constant surveillance to prevent another such deplorable event.

Not so!

Mr. Herbert Roston, former curator of the National Museum, was dismissed for negligence… And what has his successor done?

The same thing!

Nothing!

We can prove it.

Last night, at ten o'clock, an unknown man appeared at the offices of the *Washington Sun*.

At his request, he was admitted to the editor-in-chief's office. From under his coat, he produced an ebony statuette inlaid with bronze, bearing on its base the number 153.

"This statuette," he declared, "I stole from the National Museum, in the Margarita Room, earlier today.

"It isn't, truth be told, of very great value, and I could easily have taken something much more precious. But I have my reasons — which I'll explain another day — for choosing this particular piece.

"I'll leave it here for you. Display it in your window — it's worth showing off."

Having delivered these enigmatic words, the visitor placed the statuette on the editor's desk, politely bade him good evening, and left.

The statuette, number 153, is now on display in our window on Cleveland Avenue, where anyone may see it!

It can be said without fear of exaggeration that the National Museum is at least as poorly guarded as the Louvre in Paris!

The result of this article was immediate.

All day long, crowds filed past the *Washington Sun* offices to view the stolen statuette.

A swift police inquiry confirmed that the mysterious visitor had spoken the truth — and that the statuette had indeed been stolen from the National Museum.

It was returned to the museum the same day — while the editor of the *Washington Sun* was charged with receiving stolen goods.

Perhaps that's why he never dared to publish the letter he received the following morning.

A most interesting and instructive letter.

It revealed the name of the thief: John Strobbins.

And now that The Margarita is perhaps lost forever, it's with some satisfaction that one can learn exactly how the detective-burglar went about acquiring it.

Here, then, is the full text of John Strobbins's letter to the editor of the *Washington Sun*:

Sir,

Though I may have — perhaps — an exaggerated tendency to take what belongs to others (one cannot change one's nature, alas), I am nonetheless a patriot at heart.

United States forever!

I love my country. I have proved it before. And nothing that diminishes its patrimony can leave me unmoved. I shall prove it again.

The National Museum, as you know, houses glorious relics of our national independence — notably, Washington's sword, his nurse's belt buckle, a tile from his house's roof.

In my leisure hours, I take pleasure in steeping myself among these reminders of a heroic era.

So imagine my sorrow, my shock, my indignation when, on my visits to the National Museum, I saw how carelessly these noble mementos were guarded.

I resolved to teach a lesson to the negligent men entrusted with their care and — without much difficulty — took, six weeks ago, the statuette listed as number 153, representing an Indian deity.

No one noticed!

Not wanting this lesson to go unlearned, I was preparing to bring the fruit of my dexterity to your newspaper when I learned, at the same time, of the death of Jim Snowboots and of the bequest of The Margarita to the National Museum.

For some time, I had coveted this pearl — which in every respect deserves a place in my collection.

That desire, coupled with my wish to deliver a resounding lesson to the negligent custodian of our national treasures, spurred me to take possession of the beautiful Margarita.

To that end, I quietly replaced the stolen statuette back on its pedestal at the National Museum — since no one had noticed it was missing in the first place. There was no need to raise suspicions.

Then I inquired as to where The Margarita would be displayed. I learned the name of the craftsman commissioned to create the bronze pedestal meant to hold the pearl and its case.

I got myself hired as a metalworker — I have some talent in that art — and worked on that very pedestal.

I managed to conceal within the decorative moldings a secret compartment, invisible, yet large enough to hold the pearl.

That was all.

All that remained was to place it there — which proved easy, thanks to a little psychology.

Yes — psychology!

It doesn't take much reflection to understand that, on the day of President Shaft's visit, security would be virtually nonexistent. No one suspects the President of the United States!

And, besides, the curator and everyone else would have their full attention fixed on the revered President Shaft, on whom favors and promotions depend.

Thanks to some high-placed contacts, I arranged for one of my most trusted lieutenants to be hired as one of the four guards a week before the inauguration.

At the right moment — just as everyone was busy congratulating President Shaft as he made his way to the door — my man, with one swift motion, slipped the pearl into the secret compartment built into the pedestal.

I waited for the furor over The Margarita's disappearance to subside.

And three days ago, I entered the National Museum unnoticed, retrieved the pearl from its hiding place, and slipped it into my pocket.

I noted, with no little sadness, that security was no better than before.

After securing The Margarita in a safe place, I returned to the National Museum and took back statuette no. 153, which I then delivered to you.

I hope that this warning will contribute to better protection of our national treasures, and in that hope, I remain, Sir,

Yours very sincerely,

JOHN STROBBINS

P.S.

Have the pedestal examined. The compartment that held The Margarita is located under the bronze eagle clutching the American flag in its talons.

J.S.

III

The Amateur

I

For exactly three days now, Mr. John Skeeper had been staying at the Atlantic Hotel, the most luxurious in Savannah, having booked a comfortable room in advance by telegram from New York.

November had just ended, and already Savannah — with its mild climate and no snow — was filling up with chilly vacationers fleeing the harsh northern winter.

But Mr. John Skeeper was not one of them.

In the hotel register he described himself as a "man of independent means," and his conduct certainly supported that title. Unlike his neighbors, Mr. Skeeper showed nothing but disdain for the stock market quotations telegraphed daily to the hotel. No one could claim to have seen him consult the market board even once.

Mr. John Skeeper didn't even read the newspapers.

He was a tall, slender man, dressed with elegance and restraint.

Mr. John Skeeper was also not particularly sociable. Having come to Savannah, it seemed, to rest — and nothing more — he kept to himself and limited his social contributions to a polite but slightly haughty civility.

However, on the second day of his stay, Mr. Skeeper had stopped the runaway pony of Mr. Elias Mac Dowie with one strong hand, and from that moment on, a sort of familiarity arose between the two men

— meaning that whenever they met, Mr. Skeeper exchanged remarks about the weather and mutual congratulations on their respective health.

Yet Mr. Mac Dowie — a large man with a prominent belly held in by a heavy gold chain, a ruddy face crowned by a shiny bald head flanked by sandy sideburns — was worth cultivating: he was none other than the *Superintendent of the U.S. Treasury in Washington.*

But Mr. John Skeeper, having come to rest — and nothing more — seemed to care very little.

Which is why he was surprised that morning — at nine o'clock — when the steward delivering his breakfast announced:

"Sir, Mr. Mac Dowie would be much obliged if you'd visit him in his suite. He'll wait for you all morning. He says he has something important to tell you."

"Well, well…" replied John Skeeper, showing no attempt to hide his surprise. "And where does Mr. Mac Dowie live?"

"Suite 342, fourth floor."

"Very good. Tell Mr. Mac Dowie I'll be there within the hour. You may go."

Once the boy had left, Mr. Skeeper looked pensive.

As he sipped his tea, he wondered what the high official could possibly want from him — and couldn't figure it out.

He shrugged, finished his breakfast, changed from his silk pajamas into an elegant gray flannel suit, checked himself in the mirror, and left his room.

The Atlantic Hotel — a vast building fronting the sea, about two hundred meters from the shore — rose eighteen stories, served by six elevators.

Since his room was on the third floor, Mr. Skeeper saw no need to use the lift.

With a light step, he ascended the wide marble staircase and reached Suite 342.

He knocked.

"Come in!" a voice called through the door.

John Skeeper entered, crossed a tiny antechamber, and stepped into a sitting room where Mr. Mac Dowie stood smiling warmly and moved toward him.

"So kind of you to come so quickly, sir!" said the large man.

"Not at all — it's I who should thank you for the urgency with which you wanted to see me. I confess I'm anxious to know what it's about — misfortunes can happen so quickly!"

He wore an inquisitive and slightly alarmed expression.

Perhaps the official hadn't expected so direct a remark, for he looked momentarily flustered — something John Skeeper did not fail to notice.

"Oh, no need to worry. It's nothing serious. But do sit down, please!"

Mac Dowie gestured toward a low, plush chair by the window — almost too comfortable, thought John Skeeper, as though one would be completely defenseless if attacked.

"Thank you very much, Mr. Mac Dowie," Skeeper replied, "but I'm afraid my time is limited this morning. Once I know the reason you've been kind enough to summon me, I must take my leave."

"Ah, busy, are you? Always something pressing… impossible to truly rest these days…"

"Surely he didn't bring me here just to recite such banalities," thought Skeeper.

With a faint smile, he cut in:

"Perhaps it's about my business, Mr. Mac Dowie?"

"Yes — that is — no — well…"

Skeeper maintained his pleasant air.

Suddenly, the velvet curtains at the windows parted. Two burly men armed with clubs burst in and lunged at him.

"This time, John Strobbins, we've got you!" cried one of them.

"Not yet, Mollescott!"

For of course — as he'd suspected for several moments — John Skeeper was none other than John Strobbins.

He ducked just as Detective James Mollescott lunged, grabbed the policeman's ankles, and sent him crashing to the floor.

The second officer raised his club to strike the burglar-detective but never finished the swing — Strobbins headbutted him square in the face, sending him sprawling and scattering teeth across the room.

With a deft kick, Strobbins sent Mollescott, just regaining his feet, tumbling back down. Then he ran for the door.

It was locked.

Strobbins leapt back, seized the bronze bust from the mantel, and used it to smash through the mahogany panel with a resounding crash — and vanished.

Mac Dowie, who had prudently hidden in a corner when the police appeared, helped the bleeding officer back to his feet.

Though his leg was nearly dislocated, James Mollescott stood again, furious at seeing his quarry escape. He tore after Strobbins, revolver in hand.

In the corridor, he caught sight of him twenty meters ahead.

"Stop, or I'll shoot!"

Strobbins stopped — and calmly pressed the elevator button.

As the elevator arrived, Mollescott lunged at him — but Strobbins grabbed a nerve point in his arm, and the detective collapsed in pain.

In the ascending elevator, Strobbins vaulted over the cab's partition, landing at the feet of the astonished liftman. Without hesitation, he choked him out with a jiu-jitsu hold, stripped his uniform, bound his hands, and donned the gold-braided jacket and cap.

When the elevator doors opened at the eighteenth floor, Strobbins stepped out coolly, pressed the down button, and headed for the service stairwell.

Straddling the banister, he slid all the way to the ground floor, crossed the courtyard unnoticed, and reached the main entrance, where four policemen stood guard.

"Let me through," he barked.

They stepped aside without suspicion. Strobbins gave a curt salute and vanished into the street.

Minutes later, a livid Mollescott arrived, shouting:

"He was dressed as a liftman! I bet you let him through!"

The police nodded. But Strobbins was already far away — impossible to catch.

Only Elias Mac Dowie would hear from him again.

That evening, as Mac Dowie sat down to dinner, a steward informed him of a telephone call.

Still shaken, the Superintendent hurried to the phone and heard:

"Hello? Is this Elias Mac Dowie, Superintendent of the Treasury?"

"Yes."

"Well. I am John Strobbins — also known as John Skeeper. You presumed to play a contemptible little game on me this morning, forcing me to cut short my vacation. I warn you — I intend to teach you to mind your own business and to give up your ridiculous amateur-detective pretensions. You'll see soon enough. Goodbye."

Mac Dowie was too stunned to reply.

And when he finally found his voice — there was no one left on the line.

II

Mr. Elias Mac Dowie, Superintendent of the Treasury, was an eminent citizen.

Not content with serving his country by conscientiously and firmly overseeing the printing of banknotes, he also strove to exercise what he considered his natural vocation — that of discovering criminals — by offering useful advice to the police whenever he had the chance.

In truth, however, Mr. Mac Dowie had yet to deliver any brilliant proof of the keen instincts he claimed to possess.

His friends teased him good-naturedly about this.

The portly superintendent, irritated by such mockery, had recently found a way to deflect it:

"Go ahead and laugh," he'd say, "but soon enough you'll be forced to bow before my extraordinary abilities. Just you wait and see! I may *look* like I don't care about anything, and you mock what you call my impotence — ah, but patience! Mark my words: I'm working on something big — under strictest confidence, of course. I am planning nothing less than to capture the notorious John Strobbins!"

This declaration was met with widespread skepticism.

Capturing John Strobbins was easier said than done.

The famous burglar-detective had eluded and made fools of seasoned professional policemen — men far subtler than the corpulent Elias Mac Dowie.

But the superintendent, full of what he saw as his transcendent abilities, would just smile loftily and murmur:

"Time will tell."

And little by little, his unshakable confidence dulled the ridicule.

Who knew? Perhaps… perhaps… but certainly not Elias Mac Dowie himself.

For in fact he knew nothing — nothing more than any other American citizen: that John Strobbins, after stealing the magnificent Margarita pearl from the National Museum in Washington, had vanished.

That was all.

He was counting on luck.

And for once — luck was with him.

He had already been at the Atlantic Hotel for a few days when the so-called Mr. John Skeeper arrived.

Elias Mac Dowie had never seen John Strobbins except in newspaper photographs — which may or may not have been accurate.

On the first day he spotted Mr. Skeeper, he suspected nothing.

Nor on the second.

But on the third day — Mr. James Mollescott, Chief of Police in San Francisco, arrived.

Mollescott had been locked in a bitter struggle with John Strobbins for years. Time and again, the burglar-detective had slipped through his hands — even delighting in publicly humiliating him on several occasions.

Between the two men, it was open war.

Seeing that his most skillful detectives had all failed, Mollescott decided, once more, to handle it himself.

Patiently, piecing together bits of intelligence from many sources, the San Francisco police chief tracked down the fugitive. Armed with two arrest warrants — one from the Governor of California and another from the Governor of Georgia — he set out in pursuit.

Even so, Mollescott — having been outwitted so many times before — still harbored some doubt about the reliability of his information.

Not wanting to make a mistake that Strobbins would trumpet to the world, he chose to confirm the suspect's identity before moving in.

So he arrived at the Atlantic Hotel late one evening, accompanied by a brawny detective.

When they arrived, it was already 10 p.m. The false Mr. Skeeper was asleep.

But they had to move fast: confirm the man's identity and arrest him immediately.

It was delicate work — for if John Strobbins realized he was being hunted, he would certainly escape.

As Mollescott and his man sat in the hotel lobby, pondering their next move, the Chief overheard the name "Elias Mac Dowie."

Elias Mac Dowie! That settled it!

Like every policeman in America, Mollescott was aware of the superintendent's amateur-detective pretensions.

He decided to use him.

Rising from his chair, he approached the official just as Mac Dowie was heading to his suite.

In a few words, Mollescott introduced himself and secured the man's cooperation:

"If I may say so, Mr. Mac Dowie, it's almost as if I'm speaking to a colleague! Yes — yes — I'm familiar with your extraordinary abilities. And seeing you here is just further proof.

"I'm after John Strobbins — and I see you've discovered his hideout too! That's right — John Skeeper, no doubt about it. I confess I hesitated to believe he'd dare come here, and I feared I was wrong.

"But since you're on the same trail, I no longer doubt myself. Still — and I'm sure you'll agree — I feel it's my duty to see him with my own eyes. I know Strobbins and I can recognize him under any disguise.

"So I'll ask you to invite him to your suite tomorrow morning under some pretext. My man and I will hide behind the curtains, and once I've confirmed his identity, we'll quietly arrest him."

Mac Dowie puffed up with pride.

He pictured himself at his Washington club, surrounded by the envious admiration of his friends, having — he, Elias Mac Dowie — captured the elusive John Strobbins.

What a triumph!

True, the man had saved his runaway pony just days earlier — but really, should one show sentiment to such a criminal? Of course not.

Mac Dowie spoke:

"You guessed it — I've been tracking John Strobbins too! I was even planning to cable the governor to have him arrested. But since you're here, we'll share the honor of his capture!

"Come to my suite early tomorrow with your man — make sure he's strong, because our man is vigorous. I'll take care of luring him to me!"

The plan was carried out to perfection — except for one detail: the actual arrest of John Strobbins.

All day long, Mollescott — limping, furious, humiliated — had Savannah searched from end to end. His detective, meanwhile, was at the hospital having his teeth fixed.

Mac Dowie was so despondent he skipped lunch.

Worse yet, the hotel manager came to assess the damage caused by the burglar-detective and presented the following bill:

- Torn and stained Smyrna carpet: $125
- Broken mahogany door panel: $32
- Bronze bust of Madame de Lamballe, nose flattened: $500
- Import duties paid on bust: $250

TOTAL: $907.

Nine hundred and seven dollars — nearly a month's salary!

And John Strobbins was still at large.

Mac Dowie trembled with rage, pushed the paper aside, and declared curtly:

"Fine. Add it to my account. I'm leaving tomorrow."

The manager, though sorry to lose such a wealthy guest, did not press the matter.

That afternoon, Mac Dowie finally left his suite and went to the lobby.

He thought his fellow guests were watching him with mocking eyes.

For once — he was right.

He shrugged and went for a walk on the beach, regretting his disrupted vacation. A cheerful sun gleamed on the green waves and golden sand.

Clenching his fists, he muttered:

"I'll come back next year. For now, I'd better return to my post in Washington. Maybe I can pull some strings and get a raise…"

This thought cheered him slightly, and at dinner his appetite returned.

But he had scarcely finished his excellent turtle soup when the manager summoned him to the phone.

The threat of John Strobbins did its work.

The big man, flushed with emotion, returned to his table under the curious and mocking gaze of his neighbors.

He'd lost his appetite again.

Miserable John Strobbins!

The next morning, the honorable Elias Mac Dowie boarded the train for Washington, wondering what might await him.

He would not have to wait long to find out.

III

Mr. Elias Mac Dowie, Superintendent of the Central Treasury, had as his primary duty the oversight of banknote production. And it was no sinecure.

Bundles of watermark-stamped paper, trimmed to precise dimensions, were then fed through the presses and, once printed and numbered, locked away in an armored safe as impenetrable as a battleship — a safe for which Elias Mac Dowie alone held the key.

According to the Treasury's needs, the superintendent would deliver a set quantity of notes to the State Bank director, who signed and put them into circulation.

But since this official was frequently absent, he had the habit of signing a certain number of notes in advance, which then remained in Elias Mac Dowie's custody.

The very day he returned from Savannah, Mac Dowie resumed his post.

But at once his subordinates noticed a change in him.

Since the debacle at the Atlantic Hotel, the superintendent had grown somber and preoccupied, absorbed entirely in his work.

At his club he barely uttered two words an hour.

His friends — having read of his misadventure in the papers — had tried to get him to talk, without success.

They gave up.

Silent and withdrawn, Elias Mac Dowie thought more than ever about John Strobbins.

But it was no longer about catching him — oh no!

Now it was to wonder what form the burglar-detective's promised revenge might take.

Elias Mac Dowie began to lose weight.

His once-flushed cheeks grew pale and flabby...

Eight days passed this way without incident.

Mac Dowie began to regain his courage, telling himself that surely Strobbins had found more interesting things to do than pursue a grudge.

Somewhat reassured by this reasoning — and the time that had elapsed — the superintendent began thinking of how to make up the $900 his amateur detective ambitions had cost him.

How? Why, by getting a promotion!

To be named Director of the Treasury — that was the trick.

It wouldn't be easy, but Mac Dowie was confident in his abilities.

He went to the Secretary of Finance to lay out his grievances and long, loyal record of service.

The Secretary, who had no reason to be displeased with him, assured Mac Dowie that his wish would be granted soon — the current director was expected to retire shortly.

Mac Dowie left the meeting with joy in his heart.

The next day his subordinates were stunned to see his cheeks regain their color and his mouth curl back into a smile!

At the club, he even condescended to speak again, hinting to his friends that someday soon he might regale them with the true story of his dealings with John Strobbins.

They thought to themselves: *"Perhaps he's finally caught his man to be this cheerful?"*

But Mr. Mac Dowie's happiness was short-lived.

Forty-two hours, to be exact.

For at nine o'clock the next morning, arriving at his office, he sensed an unusual commotion in the Engraving and Printing workshop.

Struck by a painful premonition, he hurried there at once.

The place was in complete disarray.

Foremen and workers rushed about in a panic.

Machines stood still.

Tools lay scattered everywhere.

At the sight of the superintendent, the hubbub died and a deathly silence fell.

Elias Mac Dowie's voice rang out:

"Mr. Quincey!" he barked. "What is the meaning of this?"

The chief of production — an old, gray-haired employee — replied in a voice trembling with emotion:

"Th-the... it's the copper plate for the reverse side of the twenty-five-dollar banknotes... it's... missing!"

"You're insane, Mr. Quincey!" Mac Dowie bellowed, beside himself.

The production chief simply threw his arms heavenward.

Mac Dowie stood silent as well, staring at each worker in turn.

They all stood there, awkward and mute.

Mr. Quincey remained silent.

Unbidden, the thought of John Strobbins crept into the superintendent's mind.

But he pushed it away.

What would the burglar-detective want with a copper plate?

No, no — the plate must simply have been misplaced.

Surely, if Strobbins had wanted revenge, he would have used more decisive means.

Mac Dowie straightened his shoulders.

"This disorder is intolerable!" he pronounced. "It has gone on long enough! The result is: a plate is missing! Do you understand, Mr. Quincey? You have until this evening to find it!"

Mr. Quincey hunched his shoulders and muttered:

"I'll keep searching, Superintendent."

"You'd better!" Mac Dowie snapped. "And make it fast — and quiet! No one outside this room is to know of this ridiculous incident! Inform me the moment it's found!"

Alas, Mr. Quincey had already torn the workshop apart himself and knew full well the plate was gone.

But he bowed to his superior and said:

"You can count on me, sir."

Fuming yet dignified, Elias Mac Dowie returned to his office.

"Let's just hope this isn't one of Strobbins's tricks," he thought. *"If word of this reaches the Finance Department, my promotion is finished!"*

All day long he couldn't work.

Every sound made him jump, expecting Quincey to appear with news.

But no — five o'clock struck — closing time — and no one had come.

The situation was now serious.

Mac Dowie leapt from his chair and hurried to the workshop.

Everyone was still there.

Mr. Quincey leaned against a machine, looking utterly dejected.

Around him the workers stood, muttering wild theories.

At the sight of the superintendent, they fell silent.

"Well, Mr. Quincey?" Mac Dowie barked. "Is this how you carry out my orders? Where is the plate?"

The old man raised his hands in helplessness.

"What can I say, sir? We've searched everywhere! It's not here! And since I cannot believe that any of my men — whose honesty I vouch for — would have stolen it, I can only conclude it was taken during the night. That's most unfortunate — especially since we're about to print the new five-dollar notes!"

Mac Dowie listened without interruption, but the last sentence pushed him to the edge.

Of course he knew the plate was essential!

And now it would mean alerting the Treasury Director, perhaps even the Secretary of Finance — leading to inquiries, counter-inquiries, scandal… and goodbye to the director's chair!

He spoke slowly, with each syllable biting:

"So, Mr. Quincey — you absolutely guarantee the integrity of your staff? Absolutely? Mind your answer! I warn you: I will conduct a full and thorough investigation! And if I find negligence or a breach of regulations, I will punish it without mercy. Well?"

These harsh words seemed to steady Mr. Quincey.

"Sir," he said calmly, "I have the right, until proven otherwise, to trust my men's honesty. I have no reason to suspect them. Last night, as every night, they were thoroughly searched at the door, per regulation. I myself locked the workshop and handed the keys to the night guard. As you ordered, I've searched the place top to bottom. I have nothing to reproach myself for."

This speech only deepened Mac Dowie's rage — but he controlled himself.

"Very well," he said. "Dismiss your men — it's time. And not a word of this in town, or it will mean immediate dismissal. I'll take the necessary steps to recover the stolen item."

The workers filed out in hostile silence.

Mac Dowie left the workshop without a word to Quincey, muttering to himself:

"Surely... no doubt about it... this is a move by John Strobbins!"

Oddly, the thought did not completely dishearten him.

The damage was done — but he would fight back.

Not alone, though.

Not that he doubted his own abilities — he fancied himself a first-rate detective — but he thought some outside help might speed things along.

If he could capture Strobbins and recover the plate in one stroke, his reputation would be made!

Mac Dowie remembered receiving, a week earlier, a circular advertising the private detective agency of Brockton & Smith.

Not wanting to involve the official police — to avoid publicity — he resolved to call on Brockton & Smith, "the finest detectives in America (and therefore the world)," as their circular boasted.

Time was pressing.

Without delay, he wrote a letter summoning one of their agents to his office immediately.

After dropping it in the mail, Mac Dowie felt calmer.

He dined heartily and that night dreamt of watching a judge sentence John Strobbins to a hundred years of hard labor.

The next morning, at nine sharp, he entered his office.

At five past nine, an usher entered and handed him a card that read:

Chas Brockton of the agency, Brockton & Smith

Everywhere.

IV

"Let him in," ordered Elias Mac Dowie.

Mr. Chas. Brockton, ushered in, appeared as a stout man with a merry face framed by a thick black beard.

He waited for the door to close behind him and then said gently:

"Superintendent, my compliments! I am, from this moment, at your complete disposal!"

"Most kind of you! Please sit down… I have called you here over a very delicate matter which, as you'll understand, prevents me — by its very nature — from handling it myself with any hope of success. Otherwise—"

"Oh! Superintendent, we are well aware of your extraordinary investigative gifts! We all know how you nearly captured John Strobbins — who slipped through your fingers only because of an official policeman's blunder! Were it not for your high position, we would long ago have asked you to collaborate with us — even to lead us!"

Elias Mac Dowie puffed up at this. He was no fool, yet whenever anyone praised his illusory detective prowess, he became astoundingly gullible.

Smiling, he replied:

"Yes… I have always enjoyed this sort of work… and it is certain that many a criminal would not have escaped had I personally intervened. Well!" (Mac Dowie sighed.) "It is true I nearly caught the infamous John Strobbins. And it is certainly he who has prompted your presence here. He swore to take his revenge on me. And I strongly suspect him of being behind the disappearance of a copper plate engraved for printing banknotes, which has been missing since yesterday morning."

The superintendent then related to the detective the circumstances under which the plate's disappearance had been discovered.

Chas. Brockton, comfortably seated in a leather armchair, listened attentively, asking several precise questions along the way.

When Mac Dowie finished, Brockton sat silent a moment, lost in thought.

Finally, he said:

"It's clear the plate has indeed been stolen and carried off. Finding it again will be difficult.

"Finding the thief, however, I believe will be easy. I do not believe John Strobbins is the thief — he is a gentleman burglar who only works on a grand scale. No, I suspect it is some worker who seized the plate, hoping to use it later to produce counterfeit banknotes once the commotion has subsided.

"Fortunately, he could only take one of the two plates he would need. Which leads me to conclude that before long he will try to steal the second one. And that is when we shall catch him!"

Mac Dowie was very pleased by this reasoning.

"You and I think alike!" he said, to which Brockton nodded, flattered.

"Unfortunately, I'm in a great hurry to recover that plate, as I'll need it in a few days."

"That may still be possible," Brockton replied. "All you need to do is issue an excessively strict new set of regulations, stating they will take effect in three days. There's a very good chance our thief will rush to act before his plan becomes impossible."

"That's true… And how do you plan to operate? I don't want you letting our man slip away at any cost!"

"I am not James Mollescott, sir!" the detective said with a smile. "Where are the plates kept?"

"In a special safe whose key is held only by Mr. Quincey, head of the engraving department. Which is why I'm surprised — why didn't the thief take both plates at once? It would have been just as easy."

"Yes, but perhaps he was startled… you never know… a man committing such a risky act is very jumpy; the slightest noise terrifies him. That is probably what happened. And that would not have happened if John Strobbins were the thief — that man keeps his head!

"So I will simply need a place to hide in the engraving workshop. I'll act alone. I'll spend the night there, waiting for the thief. I have a feeling he won't be long.

"The moment I catch him, a good whack with my blackjack will bring him in alive — I'll bring him to you. We can offer him freedom in exchange for the plate's return. He won't object. And thus, without noise or scandal, we'll achieve our goal."

"And if he doesn't come?" asked Mac Dowie, nearly convinced.

"He will come — otherwise his theft would have no point. If, by some impossible chance, he hasn't come in three days, I'll redirect my investigation. But I am so sure he'll return that I will only charge my fee — two thousand dollars — if the capture happens within five days!"

At the mention of two thousand dollars, Mac Dowie grimaced slightly, but he recovered and said:

"Very well — agreed. I'll make arrangements for you to have a hiding place in the Engraving and Printing workshop.

"Come back here at four o'clock this afternoon."

"You can count on me, Superintendent! One last word: speak of our plan to no one — no one! As you know as well as I, even the smallest leak can ruin an investigation."

"I've been handling these sorts of matters long enough to know that, Mr. Brockton," Mac Dowie replied with dignity.

Chas. Brockton rose, bowed with perfect courtesy, and slowly made his way to the door and out.

Left alone, Elias Mac Dowie wasted no time.

On the spot, he drafted a new set of regulations to take effect four days later, applying to all Treasury workshop personnel.

This document anticipated the smallest lapses of discipline, doubled the number of night guards, and imposed extremely severe penalties for even the slightest carelessness.

After reading it over, the superintendent was satisfied. He rang for an usher and ordered him to take it at once to the printer to have a hundred copies made and posted everywhere the same day.

With noon approaching, pleased with himself, Elias Mac Dowie went to lunch.

Afterward, he returned to the Central Treasury and went to the Engraving and Printing workshop to find a hiding place for Chas. Brockton.

When he arrived, his new regulations — which had been posted during the lunch break — had drawn all the workers into a murmuring, indignant crowd.

At the sight of the superintendent, they immediately fell silent and scattered to their posts.

Mr. Quincey, busy examining proofs in a corner, hurried over.

"I don't like gatherings during work hours," Mac Dowie said curtly after a brisk nod. "I have issued a new regulation to strengthen discipline, which seems to me quite lax here. I hope I won't have to enforce it harshly. As for anyone who doesn't care for it, no one is forcing them to stay.

"Now, Mr. Quincey, I wish to inspect the workshop and its annexes thoroughly to consider any modifications. Please accompany me!"

Poor Mr. Quincey, stunned by this rebuke, bowed and said:

"At your disposal, Superintendent."

"Let's go."

The two men began their tour — which for Mac Dowie had only one aim: to find a hiding place for the detective.

He was soon satisfied. Near the entrance to the strongroom stood a large metal cabinet holding various tools.

Mac Dowie had it opened and saw at once that a man could easily conceal himself inside.

Pleased, he continued his inspection and returned to his office without betraying his intentions.

A few minutes later, Chas. Brockton arrived, perfectly punctual: the bronze clock on the mantel struck four as he entered.

"I've found your spot, Mr. Brockton," said Mac Dowie at once. "Near the strongroom is a cabinet where you can lie in wait quite comfortably!"

"It isn't inside the strongroom itself?"

"No — but at the entrance! The thief, if he comes, will have to pass you."

"That will do, then! Though I would have preferred to be inside the strongroom — catching the thief in the act would make his crime more serious and force a quicker confession.

"But since he will surely have his tools with him to break open the safe, I'll just let him get to work... and take him at the right moment."

"Exactly. But don't let him damage the safes — I don't want any scandal, as I've told you."

"I'll handle it. At the first scratch on the safe's wall, I'll stop him! I've thought of everything.

"Now, I just need a written authorization from you allowing me to stay in the workshop tonight. A guard making his rounds could discover me — and if I had no document proving my presence was authorized, the very scandal you wish to avoid would erupt... you understand."

Mac Dowie did not answer at once. After a moment's thought, he conceded the point.

He took Treasury letterhead and wrote:

For surveillance purposes, I authorize Mr. Charles Brockton, private detective, to remain in the Engraving and Printing workshop and adjacent areas during the night of December 5–6. Mr. Brockton is to report to no one but myself.

Washington, December 5

Elias Mac Dowie

Superintendent of the Central Treasury.

"There," said the superintendent, handing the paper to the detective, who carefully tucked it into his wallet.

V

"Now then," said Elias Mac Dowie, "all we have to do is wait for the workers to leave. Then I'll take you to your hiding place. Have you eaten?"

"No, but I have something to eat and drink in my pockets! I planned everything!"

"All right then! So we wait… Cigar?"

"With pleasure, Superintendent!"

The two men lit gold-banded cigars from an armorial box the superintendent took out of his desk. They smoked in silence, each lost in his own thoughts…

At six o'clock sharp, Elias Mac Dowie judged the time had come. The last worker had long since left, and the vast Treasury buildings were now utterly silent.

The superintendent rose and said:

"If you're ready, Mr. Brockton, I'll show you to your hiding place. Wait here a moment while I fetch the keys."

"At your service, Superintendent," the detective replied.

After glancing to make sure all his drawers and cabinets were locked — for he was a cautious man — the superintendent left.

Alone, Brockton drew a tiny keyring from his pocket, quickly unlocked one of the desk drawers, slipped in a slim package wrapped in paper, shut the drawer again with a sly smile, and went back to his chair.

Five minutes later the door opened. Elias Mac Dowie appeared, holding a ring of gleaming nickel-plated keys. With a nod, he invited the detective to follow him.

They crossed empty corridors, a vast courtyard, a little antechamber, and stopped at a thick oak door.

"Here we are: the Engraving and Printing workshop!" said Mac Dowie. "Come along."

Brockton obeyed, and at last they reached the metal cabinet near the entrance to the strongroom.

"Here's your lodging for the night!" said Mac Dowie with a smile. "Not very comfortable, but—"

"You don't earn two thousand dollars playing the banjo, that's for sure," Brockton grinned. "It's just a few nights, after all… And where is the strongroom?"

"That door there — yes, that's it. From inside the cabinet, slightly ajar, you'll see everything."

"Indeed… Do you have the key to the strongroom?"

"No, it's kept in a special box, and only the head engraver has the key… Need anything else?"

"No. Just don't lock me in — or if you must, for the guards' sake, leave me the workshop key. Fires happen quickly, and I've no desire to roast alive!"

"Good point! The first round comes at 6:35. I'd forgotten! I'll leave you the key — return it tomorrow. Lock up behind me."

"Agreed," said Brockton, pocketing the key Mac Dowie detached from his ring.

"Good luck then — and don't delay getting into your cabinet, the guards will be here soon!"

"Don't worry, Superintendent."

With that, Elias Mac Dowie left. Night had fallen completely, and only the pale glow of the electric courtyard lamps shone through the barred workshop windows.

Brockton locked the door behind Mac Dowie, then — silent as a cat — slipped into the cabinet among the tools and pulled the door closed.

Ten minutes later the patrol arrived: two guards with lanterns and revolvers. They searched thoroughly and left, seeing nothing amiss.

From his hiding place, Brockton had watched everything.

Once the door closed, he emerged and smiled silently.

"Now to work," he murmured.

The next morning, after a hearty breakfast, Elias Mac Dowie was preparing to leave his 26th Street home for his office when his valet burst into the dining room, flushed with excitement.

"Sir! There are two gentlemen here, detectives, insisting they must speak to you at once!"

"That's it," thought Mac Dowie, "Brockton and Smith, here to report the thief's capture. Truly clever, those detectives…"

"Show them in," he told the valet.

"Very good, sir."

He glanced at the clock: 8:30. Plenty of time.

But when the door opened, neither man resembled Chas. Brockton.

"Gentlemen," said Mac Dowie, "you wished to see me? How can I help?"

"Mr. Mac Dowie," one replied, "we're here on behalf of the Attorney General. I am Inspector Martins; this is Detective Fourner.

"This morning at six, the Treasury night guards discovered that the strongroom holding the finished banknotes had been breached. The armored door was cut open with an acetylene torch. Three of the six safes were also broken into. The Attorney General asks you to come immediately to assess the loss."

Mac Dowie's face went through every color of the rainbow — ending in a deep brick red. He had to clutch the table to keep from collapsing.

He understood now. He'd been played — thoroughly! Brockton was an agent of John Strobbins!

"I… I'll come at once, gentlemen," he stammered.

Unsteady, he climbed into a carriage to the Central Treasury.

Pandemonium reigned there. The Attorney General — an imposing, clean-shaven old man — motioned him over, holding a sheet of paper.

"What's the meaning of this, sir?" he demanded, showing it to Mac Dowie.

It was the pass Mac Dowie himself had written for Chas. Brockton.

"This is your signature, isn't it? Then you'll explain why you wrote this. The man who presented it left the Treasury at four this morning — and he's the one who gutted the safes!

"Come with me. Let's assess the damage."

Head bowed, Mac Dowie followed him to the strongroom.

Three safes stood gaping open. In a glance, Mac Dowie saw the devastation: about twenty bundles of watermark paper for $100 notes gone, and — far worse — ten thousand signed, numbered, ready-to-circulate $100 bills missing.

"One million dollars," he murmured.

"That's what we thought," said the Attorney General. "I regret to say I must place you under arrest."

"But I'm innocent! Let me explain—"

But his rage and despair rendered him incoherent.

Two detectives cuffed him and led him away amid general astonishment.

Even after regaining his composure, Mac Dowie failed to convince the examining magistrate of his innocence.

The Brockton & Smith Agency had never received his letter. No one there knew anything of this affair.

Even worse, the missing copper plate was found in Mac Dowie's own office desk drawer.

The case against him was overwhelming. He was sent before the assizes.

His trial was swift. So damning was the evidence that even his own lawyer advised him to plead guilty.

As the judge prepared to pronounce sentence, a courthouse guard handed him a letter.

The judge opened it and read:

Sir,

It is the accomplice — or rather, the man you *think* is the accomplice — of Mr. Elias Mac Dowie who writes. Mr. Mac Dowie is innocent. And if he stands before you now, it is for having meddled in what did not concern him.

An employee of the Treasury, he fancied himself a policeman and tried to arrest me — John Strobbins, gentleman burglar.

Had it not been for the bumbling of one James Mollescott, head of San Francisco's police, he might have succeeded. Because of him, I had to cut short my winter holiday in Savannah.

I resolved to teach him to be more modest — and above all, more cautious.

I arranged for one of my associates, a Treasury worker (I have friends everywhere), to steal a copper plate. Knowing Mac Dowie aspired to become director of the Treasury, I knew he would keep the theft quiet while frantically seeking to recover the missing plate.

My man smuggled the plate out in the sole of his shoe.

Meanwhile, having sent Mac Dowie a circular from a certain well-known detective agency (where, naturally, I also have friends), I came to him in disguise when he called for help.

I slipped the missing plate into his desk drawer and convinced him to hide me in the engraving workshop. From there, using tools I'd brought for the purpose, it was child's play to open the safes.

But I won't waste more of your valuable time.

You know the rest.

James Mollescott can vouch for my identity.

Yours most respectfully,

John Strobbins,

Gentleman Burglar.

An hour later, the trial resumed. Elias Mac Dowie was acquitted — but found to have acted with recklessness and imprudence.

He was ordered to pay court costs and dismissed from his post.

And, in a cruel irony, now that Elias Mac Dowie was free to pursue police work full time, he no longer had any desire to.

He was no longer an *amateur*…